Mine's a Winner

GRAFFIX

356442

First paperback edition 2001
First published 2000 in hardback by
A & C Black (Publishers) Ltd
35 Bedford Row, London WC1R 4JH

Text copyright © 2000 Michael Hardcastle
Illustrations copyright © 2000 Bob Moulder
Cover illustration © 2000 Mike Adams

ISBN 0-7136-5353-1

A CIP catalogue for this book is available from the
British Library.

Printed and bound in Spain by G. Z. Printek, Bilbao

Mine's a Winner

Michael Hardcastle
Illustrated by Bob Moulder

A & C Black · London

Chapter One

Tex and Stamp were old friends.

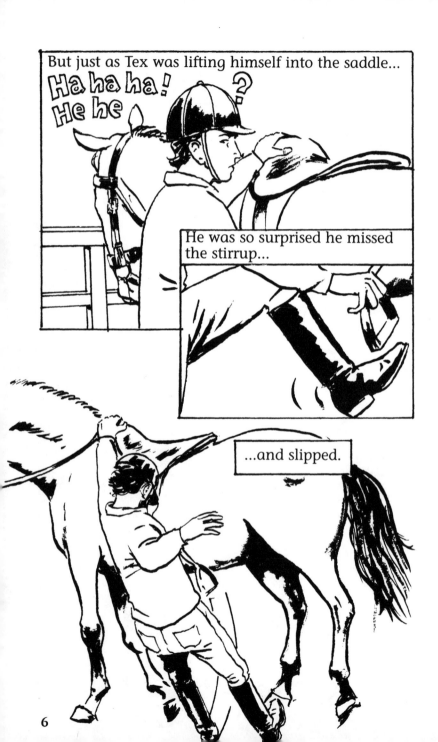

7

The girl wasn't going to let the subject alone because it was amusing her friend so much.

9

He really hadn't expected them to accept his invitation; he guessed they'd find an excuse to disappear now they'd had a good laugh.

He led the way into the Speed Horse Centre. Then he wished he'd invited them to go ahead of him so he could admire Sadie's legs again.

13

Chapter Two

The mechanical horse looked the business. It was mounted on a special support. When switched on it would buck and tilt, rear and dip. It could also gallop at a fearful speed. Tex went through the complete range of movements and always looked comfortable.

15

You just go on enjoying yourself — on your own. If you're going to be a jockey you must learn not to fall off.

That made him angry.

I don't fall off and I'm not going to be a jockey. I'm going to train racehorses. That's the way to make money. I'll be my own boss. My runners will all be winners.

He'd tried his best to detain them but they'd gone.
If they had horses they weren't riding them. They
were on bicycles, which showed off Sadie's legs.

When Tex reached
home he was still in
a bad mood.

As he went into the kitchen he bumped into his younger brother, Kyle.

Don't get in my way!

What's biting you? Fall off your horse, did you?

How d'you know that? Has that girl rung up here?

Even before he said it, Tex knew he was being stupid. But now he had to explain to Kyle what he meant.

Although his brother could be a pain, Tex liked him and they got on well. Tex said what had happened.

I still don't know what set them off laughing. Worse, I don't know anything at all about Sadie except her name.

Well, if she's into horses you're bound to see her around again.

Tex hoped so. He just knew he wanted to see her again, see her and talk to her and convince her he wasn't the idiot she seemed to think he was.

Chapter Three

A week later Tex was exercising a horse for a neighbouring farmer, Matt Morgan. It was a jumper that Mr Morgan hoped to ride in a point-to-point race, so he needed it to be as fit as possible. Tex rode out for the farmer quite often and enjoyed the chance to work with different horses.

Come on, Peak Time, show us how good you are!

Peak Time's ears pricked,

he increased his speed...

22

...then soared over the training fence.

It was just as Tex was turning...

Sadie ?!

He didn't signal that he'd seen her. Already he'd decided he'd show her how good he was at taking a horse over a jump. Tex urged Peak Time on...

Turn, turn!

...forgetting the horse lived up to his name. He liked to take his time, to jump only when he was ready.

Tex yanked at the horse's head again, kicked him on with his heels and urged into his ear.

Go, go, GO!

25

Peak Time went, but only in his own way.

He wasn't ready for the fence but he was too close to miss it out.

So he jinked sideways.

Then he tried to correct himself as the fence loomed up.

At the last moment he
whipped sideways again –

THUD

Tex was furious with himself, and furious with the horse. He might even have slapped him if Peak Time hadn't galloped out of range.

Clap

But then...

Clap- Clap-

...politely
but
firmly.

Of course, it was Sadie. Somehow, it sounded more insulting than her laughter.

Clap- Clap

ap

It was you who startled the horse. He wasn't expecting to see you standing there. It took his eye off the obstacle.

Nonsense!

I've been standing here ages. The horse had seen me even if you hadn't. So –

Hey, lad, what d'you think you're doing – with my horse?

Oh, sorry, Mr Morgan. Didn't know you were watching.

Not surprised.

Don't think you know half of what you're supposed to be doing. I always said someone daft enough to give himself a cowboy name would end up in trouble one day. Well, I'm not having you ride my horses like a cowboy. They need understanding and a good pair of hands.

I just made one mistake, Mr Morgan. That's all.

Before Tex could plead for another chance Matt Morgan urged Peak Time into a canter and they headed off to the stables.

Tex was horrified. He had just lost a job that meant a lot to him. Apart from the money he earned, it gave him a chance to ride a variety of horses. How would he get to be a racehorse trainer if he couldn't even hold this job down?

You see what you've done? That wouldn't have happened if you hadn't been here.

Hey, don't blame me!

He knew he was being unfair but he couldn't help it. He'd met Sadie only twice and both times she'd made him look like a fool.

I didn't do anything but watch you ride. Or try to ride. Anyway, what d'you mean by telling that man I'm your girlfriend? I'm nothing of the sort and you know it.

Tex was so annoyed at losing his job he'd forgotten the embarrassing remark.

That was his idea, not mine. I've never mentioned you to anyone.

That wasn't quite true but he didn't think his talk with Kyle counted.

Anyway, how did you know I was here, riding out for Mr Morgan? Or did you just happen to be passing?

Oh, I'm not getting into that stupid conversation.

She had parked her bike beside a post and moments later was riding away at a furious speed.

34

Tex's own temper didn't improve as he made his way home. Only thoughts of spending more time with Stamp kept him from kicking something. But he couldn't keep Sadie out of his mind. He felt sure horses meant as much to her as they did to him. So they should have got on fine.

If only they had a chance to get to know one another.

Chapter Four

In the lounge Tex slumped into a chair.

Hi, Mum.

Consonant please, Carol.

H.

Did that girl get hold of you?

What girl?

The one who rang here just after you'd gone to Mr Morgan's.

Another consonant.

W.

37

Tex went off to the stables to groom Stamp.

Listen, Stamp, what d'you think of this?

There's this gorgeous girl who wants to get to know me. Must do because she remembered my name and found my phone number. Aren't you impressed? I am.

40

But when Tex started to ask around at the Centre no one could help him. A couple of people thought they remembered her because she was good-looking. The manager thought Ali had been in.

She's a bit of a giggler, isn't she? The brunette.

No one, though, could provide an address or telephone number.

As he rode home, Tex began to think he'd never see Sadie again. After all, she'd seen him fall twice. On top of that she'd heard him being sacked from his part-time job. In her eyes, he was a loser. And he didn't think Sadie was the sort of girl who'd go for a loser.

Tex was desperate to be a winner. He knew he could ride as well as almost anyone. He was certain he could work with horses because he understood them. Ever since he was small he'd studied horses and learned all he could about them. That's why he wanted to train them. He was going to turn them into winners.

All he needed now was a chance to show Sadie what he could really do.

43

To cheer himself up, Tex stopped at a greengrocer's and bought Stamp a bag of carrots. Stamp loved them more than any other treat. It made Tex smile just to see the way the sleek roan crunched them. The smile faded when he got home because there was no message from Sadie. And in the week that followed nobody could come up with any idea about how he might find her.

But one day Tex was in the village...

That's Ali!

45

Hi, I'd like to see you about something.

She sounded business-like.

Oh, sure.

Tex agreed without asking what she had in mind. The fact that she wanted to see him was enough.

I'll meet you at the Speed Horse place in half an hour. I'll be riding Harvest. He's my cross-country horse. See you.

The phone went down before he could say another word. As he hurriedly tacked-up Stamp his heart began to pound. Crazy! He'd never felt like this before. What was wrong with him? He couldn't believe how desperate he was to see Sadie again.

Chapter Five

Harvest was a bay with unusual white markings on his face but Tex paid little attention to him.

He nodded and for some minutes they rode silently side by side.

But eventually Tex felt he had to say something.

52

53

Sadie took off her helmet and stared at Tex.

I've asked around and people say you are good. I talked to Mr Morgan. He says your only problem is you like to show off.

By the way, he'll let you ride his horses again if you ask politely and promise to be sensible.

Hey, I don't need anyone to do my talking for me!

If I want to ride for somebody I'll do the asking. So –

Tex, calm down!

I'm on your side. Listen, I just want to ask if you'd like to ride in a cross-country event with me on Sunday.

Ali says you can ride her horse if you want. Then you can show me how good you are with different horses. I'd also like to have someone with me.
How about it?

Tex was totally surprised by the suggestion. Somehow it didn't ring true. Was he being set up for something?

Why can't Ali be there? I mean, if she fancies me like you say, she should be eager.

Stamp jinked sideways, half-reared and then tried to spin round.

Tex reined in and got as close as possible to the frightened horse's ears. It looked as if he were trying to swallow them.

Easy, boy. Easy.

Very impressive, the way you handled that. You had an excuse this time to fall off but you didn't.

Tex, pleased to have won praise from her, just grinned.

They rode on, up the hill, and talked about horses and cross-country events. Tex kept hoping she'd say something else about him but she didn't. He told her about his ambition to become a racehorse trainer and win big races.

When they returned to the Speed Horse Centre she asked him again if he'd ride Red Rascal on Sunday. He'd made up his mind the moment she asked him but he didn't let on immediately.

I think I might. But I want to know something first:

Do you fancy me?

She looked at him and he thought her face was pinker than usual.

Her reply, though, gave nothing away.

I'd not tell you that, would I, even if I did? A girl has to have her secrets.

Tex was delighted. She hadn't said no, which was what he'd expected. So maybe she even felt as strongly about him as he felt about her. But when he tried to get closer to her, she edged Harvest away.

So, will you be there on Sunday?

You couldn't keep me away even with a shotgun!

Chapter Six

There was nothing reddish about Red Rascal's colouring, Tex discovered on Sunday. Ali's horse was almost jet black and showed a lot of the whiteness of his eyes as he allowed Tex to tighten his girths. He seemed to have lots of spirit and was on his toes from the moment his rider took the reins.

Tex knew then that was why Ali wanted him to ride her horse. He was probably too hard a ride for a slim young girl. Tex leaned over and whispered calming words into Rascal's ears.

And the nervy horse settled at once.

You'll have to teach Ali that trick.

I'd rather teach you.

Sadie just smiled and moments later they were testing their horses at the obstacles before the cross-country event started.

Tex found that Red Rascal didn't mind jumping uphill.

But he was very nervous about going down any slope.

Certainly he didn't like splashing through water. Several times Tex had to whisper into his long ears to get him to do as he was told.

She swung Harvest away to jump a log on top of a steep bank.

But the bay refused.

Twice more she tried
without success.

Tex cantered across to her.

I'll try my magic trick on him.

And before Sadie could stop him he'd leaned over, grasped Harvest's ear and spoke urgently.

Calm down, boy, calm down!

Instead of calming down, Harvest shot
away like a bullet from a gun.

He moved so fast Tex was
almost jerked from his saddle.

By the time he'd recovered control of Red Rascal, Sadie's horse was running away with her.

It was plain she couldn't stop him.

Go, boy, go!

He knew he had to catch her before there was a disaster.

Harvest, however, swerved. That chance was gone.

Faster, faster!

Tex dug his heels into Rascal's flanks. And the black horse responded.

Spectators had stopped to watch Tex and Sadie.

The crowd realised they had nothing to cheer about.
If they hit the stone wall they might be killed.

Tex yelled for a last burst of speed as Rascal drew level with Harvest. He eased his feet from the stirrups. There was only one way to stop the runaway horse now.

Tex flung himself at Rascal's head, trying to grasp the reins at the same time.

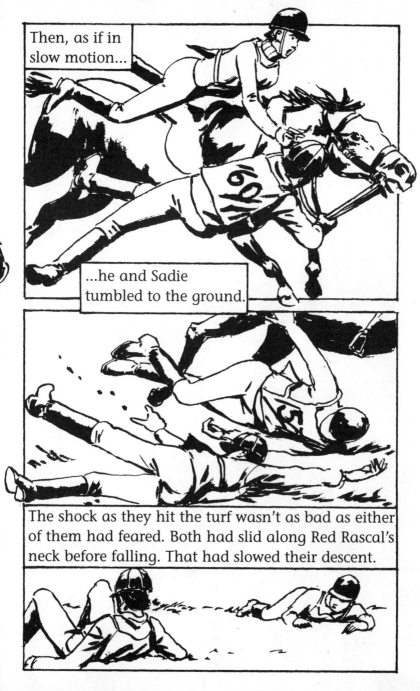

Then, as if in slow motion...

...he and Sadie tumbled to the ground.

The shock as they hit the turf wasn't as bad as either of them had feared. Both had slid along Red Rascal's neck before falling. That had slowed their descent.

And then she kissed him.